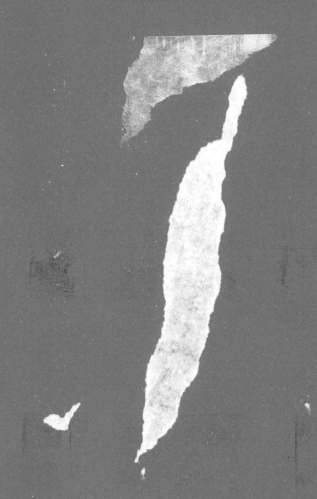

Apple Pie

art by Gennady Spirin

vwm

PHILOMEL BOOKS

A a

A, a, Apple Pie

B b

B, b. Bit it.

C c

C, c. Cut it.

Dd

E e

E, e. Eats it.

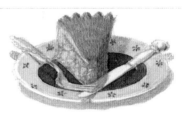

F f F, f. Fought for it.

Gg *G, g. Got it.*

H h

H, h. Had it.

I i

I, i. Inspected it.

J j

I, j. Jumped for it.

Kk
K, k. Knelt for it.

L l

L, l. Longed for it.

Mm

M, m. Mourned for it.

N n

N, n. Nodded for it.

O o   *O, o. Opened it.*

P p P.p. Peeped in it.

Qq Qq. Quartered it.

R r

R, r. Ran for it.

S s *S, s. Sang for it.*

T t

T, t. Took it.

U u

U, u. Upset it.

V v

V, v. Viewed it.

W w

W, w. Wanted it.

Xx

X, x. All had a large slice.

Y y Y *Y, y. And went*

off to bed. Z, z. z Z

A Apple Pie is a traditional English alphabet nursery rhyme that can be traced back at least to 1671, when it was quoted in the writings of theologian John Eachard. Since then, many variations have been published, most famously Kate Greenaway's illustrated edition in 1886. Back then, the letters "I" and "J" were often used interchangeably, so there was no separate page for the letter "I"; however, to reflect the modern alphabet, this version of *A Apple Pie* includes the letter "I."

Patricia Lee Gauch, editor

PHILOMEL BOOKS
A division of Penguin Young Readers Group
Published by The Penguin Group
Penguin Group (USA) Inc., 375 Hudson Street, New York, NY 10014, U.S.A.
Penguin Group (Canada), 10 Alcorn Avenue, Toronto, Ontario, Canada M4V 3B2 (a division of Pearson Penguin Canada Inc.)
Penguin Books Ltd, 80 Strand, London WC2R 0RL, England.
Penguin Ireland, 25 St. Stephen's Green, Dublin 2, Ireland (a division of Penguin Books Ltd.)
Penguin Group (Australia), 250 Camberwell Road, Camberwell, Victoria 3124, Australia (a division of Pearson Australia Group Pty Ltd).
Penguin Books India Pvt Ltd, 11 Community Centre, Panchsheel Park, New Delhi - 110 017, India.
Penguin Group (NZ), Cnr Airborne and Rosedale Roads, Albany, Auckland 1310, New Zealand (a division of Pearson New Zealand Ltd).
Penguin Books (South Africa) (Pty) Ltd, 24 Sturdee Avenue, Rosebank, Johannesburg 2196, South Africa.
Penguin Books Ltd, Registered Offices: 80 Strand, London WC2R 0RL, England.

Library of Congress Cataloging-in-Publication Data
A apple pie / Gennady Spirin.   p. cm.
Summary: Introduces the letters A to Z while following the fortunes of an apple pie.
1. Nursery rhymes. 2. Alphabet rhymes. 3. Children's poetry. [1. Nursery rhymes. 2. Alphabet.] I. Spirin, Gennadii, ill.
PZ8.3.A5567 2005   [E]—dc22   2004030497

ISBN 0-399-23981-2
1 3 5 7 9 10 8 6 4 2
First Impression